George
and
Martha
Two Great
Friends

For George and Cecille

The stories in this book were originally published by Houghton Mifflin Company in *George and Martha.*

www.hmhco.com

First Green Light Readers edition 2010

The Library of Congress Cataloging-in-Publication Data is on file.
ISBN: 978-0-618-96178-8 hardcover
ISBN: 978-0-547-40625-1 paperback

Manufactured in China
SCP 10 9 8 7 6 5 4 3
4500463728

written and illustrated by

JAMES MARSHALL

sandpiper

Green Light Readers

HOUGHTON MIFFLIN HARCOURT

BOSTON NEW YORK

THREE
STORIES ABOUT
TWO GREAT
FRIENDS
THE TUB

STORY NUMBER
ONE

George was fond of peeking in windows.

One day George peeked in on Martha.

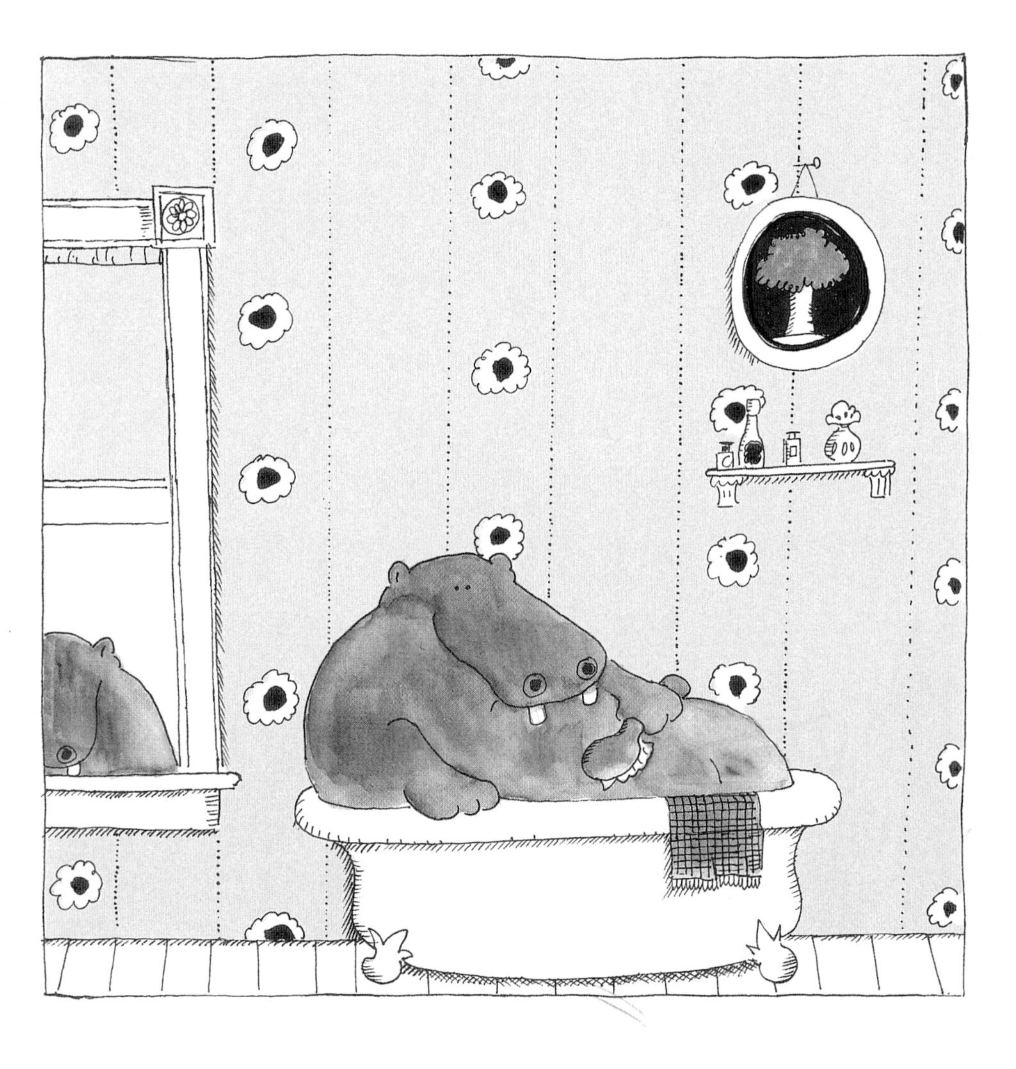

He never did that again.
"We are friends," said Martha. "But there is such a thing as privacy!"

STORY
NUMBER
TWO

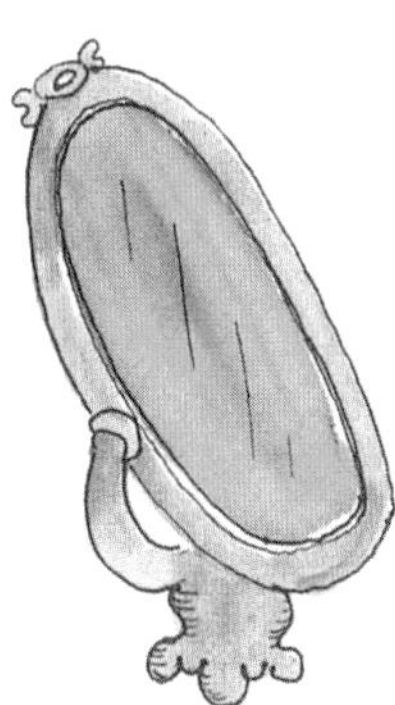

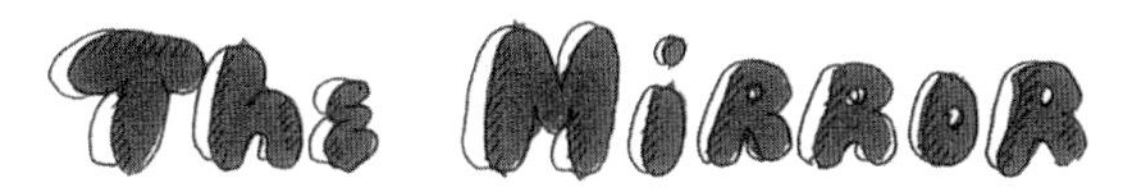
The Mirror

"How I do love to look at myself in the mirror," said Martha. Every chance she got, Martha looked at herself in the mirror.

Sometimes Martha even woke up
during the night to look at herself.
"This is fun." She giggled.

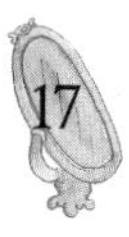

But George was getting tired of watching Martha look at herself in the mirror.

One day George pasted a silly picture he had drawn of Martha onto the mirror.

What a scare it gave Martha. "Oh dear!" she cried. "What has happened to me?"

"That's what happens when you look at yourself too much in the mirror," said George.

"Then I won't do it ever again," said Martha.

And she didn't.

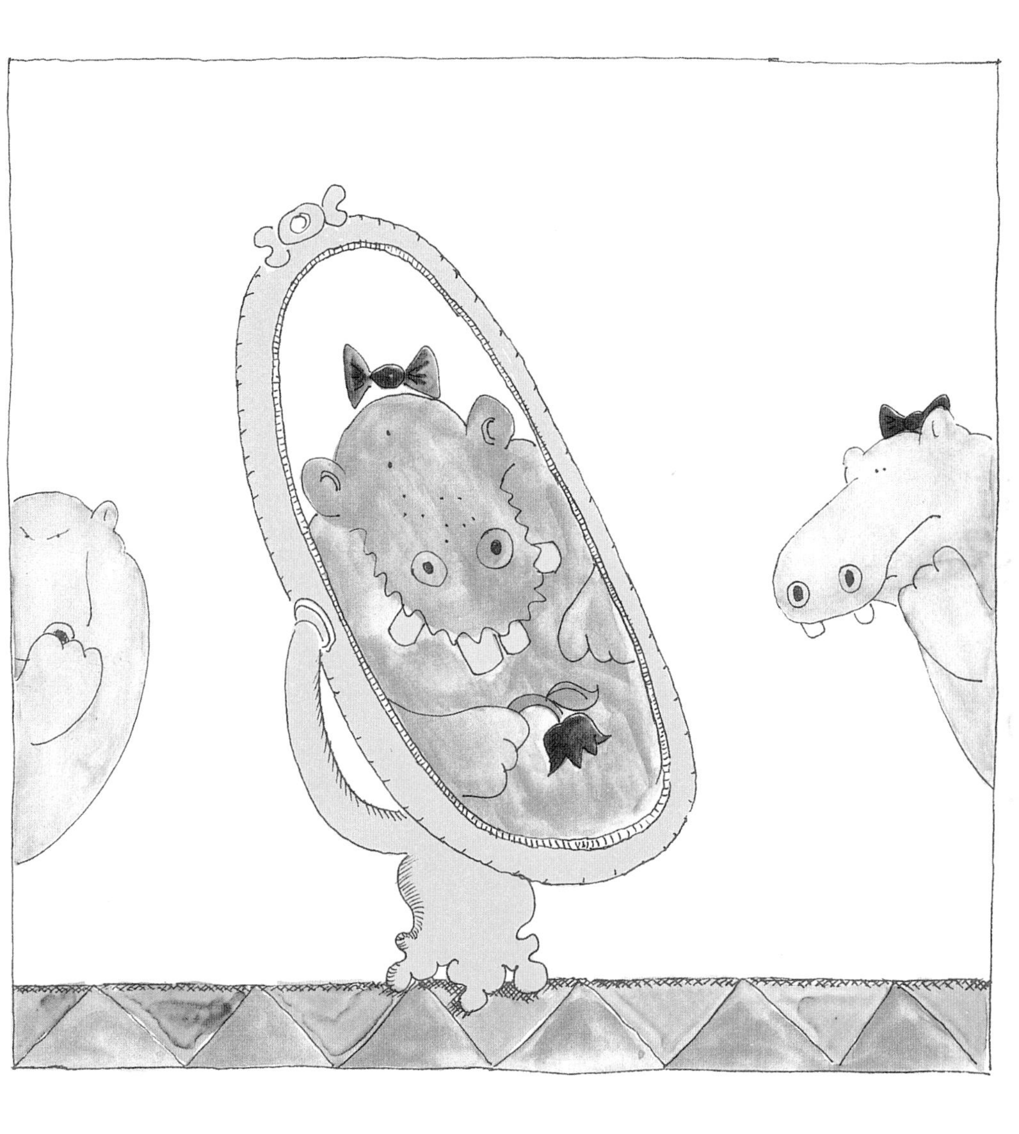

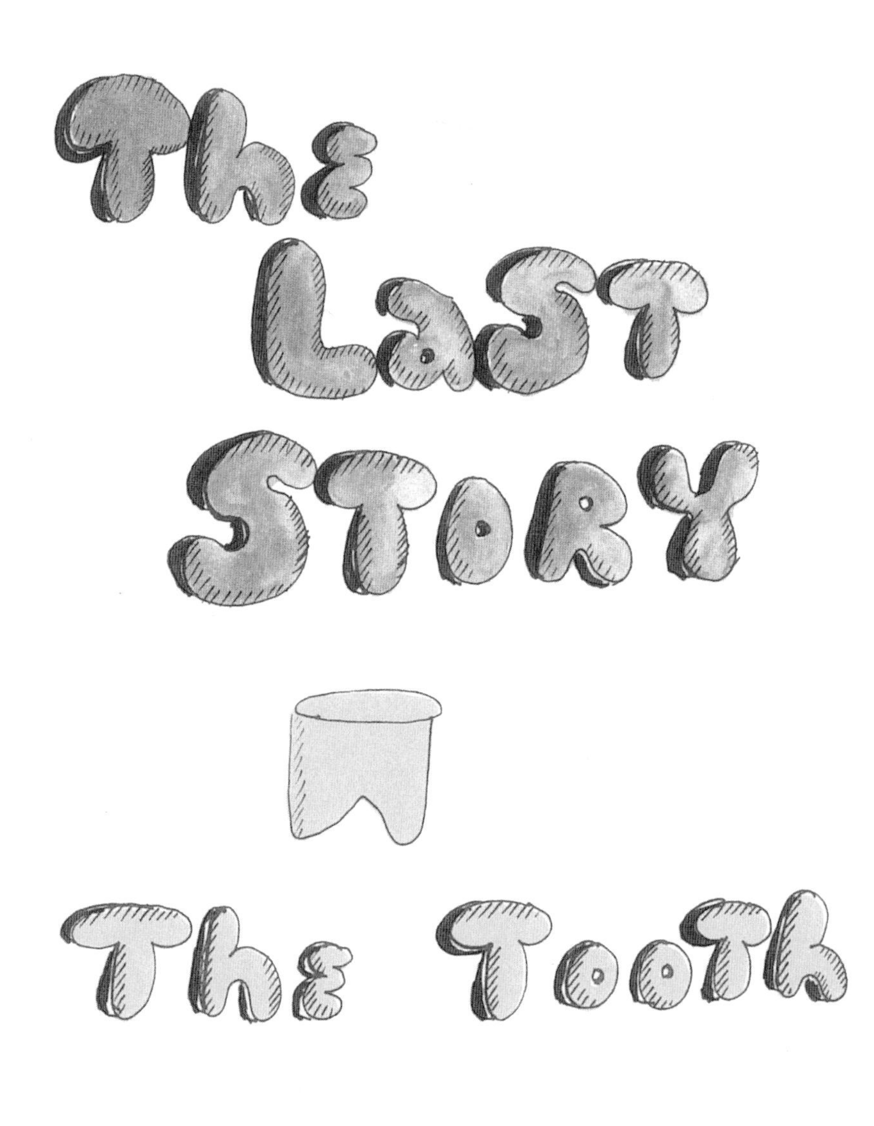
The Last Story
The Tooth

One day when George was skating to
Martha's house, he tripped and fell.
And he broke off his right front tooth.
His favorite tooth too.

When he got to Martha's, George cried his eyes out. "Oh dear me!" he cried. "I look so funny without my favorite tooth!"

"There, there," said Martha.

The next day George went to the dentist. The dentist replaced George's missing tooth with a lovely gold one.

Buck
Mc TOOTH
D.D

When Martha saw George's lovely new golden tooth, she was very happy.

"George!" she exclaimed. "You look so handsome and distinguished with your new tooth!"

And George was happy too. "That's what friends are for," he said. "They always look on the bright side and they always know how to cheer you up."

"But they also tell you the truth," said Martha with a smile.

Crossword Puzzle

Use clues from "The Tub," "The Mirror," and "The Tooth" to fill in the puzzle! Answers at the bottom of the page.

Across

1. What Martha needs when she's taking a bath.
2. What Martha likes to see herself in.
3. The color of George's new tooth.

Down

1. What Martha told George when he showed her his new tooth.
2. What George was doing when he fell and broke his tooth.

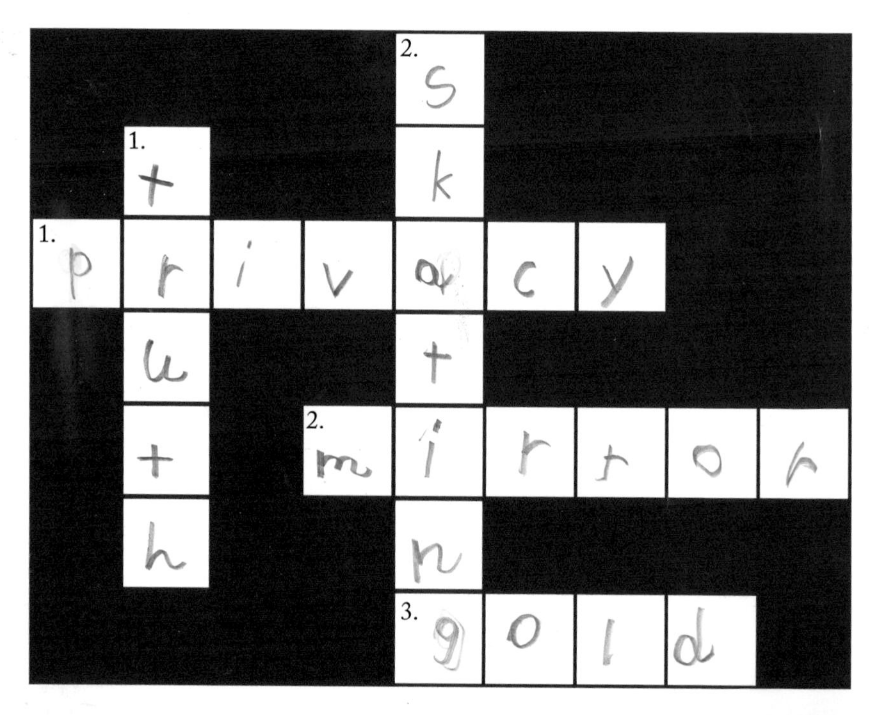

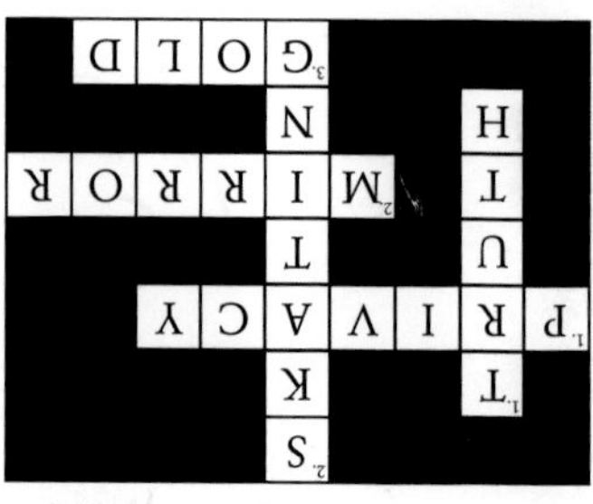

Cryptogram

Unscramble the letters! Answers at the bottom of the page.

1. What George is doing in windows.

   EKIGPE**N**

2. What Martha did when she looked at herself in the mirror. **D**LIGGEG

3. The kind of picture George drew of Martha.

   LY**I**LS

4. What George did right before he broke his tooth.

   DIPTE**R**P

5. How George thought he looked without his tooth. YUN**F**N

6. The kind of gold tooth George got. VOYL**E**L

Magic Word: Unscramble the **BOLD** letters to find the magic word!

1.Peeking 2. Giggled 3. Silly 4. Tripped 5. Funny 6. Lovely

Magic Word: Friend

More fun activities to do at home!

Draw a picture of yourself and your best friend in a flying machine.

Draw a silly picture of yourself.

Write a story about the first time you lost a tooth. Did it just fall out or did you have an accident like George? What kind of new tooth would you like if you could choose? Draw a picture!